Haikus for Punsters

Haikus for Punsters

Paul Treatman

iUniverse, Inc.
New York Lincoln Shanghai

Haikus for Punsters

iUniverse books may be ordered through booksellers or by contacting:

iUniverse
2021 Pine Lake Road, Suite 100
Lincoln, NE 68512
www.iuniverse.com
1-800-Authors (1-800-288-4677)

ISBN-13: 978-0-595-39271-1 (pbk)
ISBN-13: 978-0-595-67682-8 (cloth)
ISBN-13: 978-0-595-83668-0 (ebk)
ISBN-10: 0-595-39271-7 (pbk)
ISBN-10: 0-595-67682-0 (cloth)
ISBN-10: 0-595-83668-2 (ebk)

Printed in the United States of America

Acknowledgements

Thank you, Sylvia Rubin, your love and devotion are my *raison d'etre*.

Two literary works, over time, provided the inspiration for "Haikus for Punsters." Years ago, I came across "PUN-ishment" by Harvey C. Gordon. I really enjoyed your collection, Mr. Gordon. More recently, my son Scott and his wife Linda gifted me with "Haikus for Jews" by David M. Butler. Brilliant, Mr. Butler. Then Eureka struck me. Suddenly I felt I could prepare a "coffee table" book, one that marries the haiku to the pun. And then the pun-imbedded haikus kept pouring out of me for weeks. My thanks for their indulgence and suggested offerings go to Sylvia Rubin, Bernard Gutstsadt, Muriel Taylor and Chuck Farber. Not only them but to the myriad friends and colleagues who through the decades tolerated, even with sourpussed reactions, the punning I inflicted upon them.

Dedication

To Abbe Jo and Jeffery, Scott and Linda,
Melissa and Bryon, Jennifer and Anthony
and all their progeny, extant and future.

AND

To the cherished memory of
Elaine Treatman, who started it all.

Foreword

The haiku is a very old Japanese verse form that attempts to express cogently a thought in an economical three lines of 5 syllables, 7 syllables and 5 syllables. The haiku form has flowered in recent decades among poets as well as school children nationwide.

In this little book, I have melded the haiku form with the pun—a form of humor considered lowly by many. Not I. I have always loved and used puns, especially when I wanted to get thrown out of parties that bore me.

Puns have been used by poets, including Shakespeare, even before the haiku appeared. The pun is a word or expression that is a play on words. The pun might be a word with a double meaning within the context of the thought expressed. It might be a word that by design almost sounds like another word different from the word that the listener or reader might have expected. It might be a two-word expression whose first letters have been transposed for hopefully comic effect. Mrs. Malaprop's malapropisms were puns.

All of these haikus are mine. Most of the embedded puns are mine. A few puns I appropriated from the general domain and the chatter from cyberspace, and then I wove them into haikus. This is a literary marriage that I hope will entertain you.

Feel free to use the puns, if you dare, whether inside or outside the haikus. Also, try writing the little verses, not necessarily pun-imbedded, as challenging fun.

Archeologist

Carts away ancient treasures,

Returns to his digs.

Restaurant diner,

Thinking of wife's cooking skills,

Orders a roast pot.

Paul Treatman

Toothless man goes to

Dentist, who examines, treats

Him for chewing gum.

Jews once vacationed

In Catskills' Borscht Belt, launching

Beet generation.

Paul Treatman

Old unwashed seamstress

Never performs ablutions—

Filthy sew and sew!

Dowager enters

Beauty parlor and demands

Hairdo to dye for.

Boasting huge sales spike,

Condom manufacturer

Is stretching the point.

Rudy Vallee helps

Date set the table, then sings

My tine is your tine.

Paul Treatman

Chinese chef begins

Lessons in American

Dance with Wok and Roll.

Settler's lad asks dad:

Is Egyptian belly dance

A new Gaza Strip?

Devour oatmeal, grits,

Corn flakes, bran. Be a

Cereal killer.

Graduate becomes

Professional fisherman

With poor net income.

Paul Treatman

Rich socialites love

Apple pie. They do enjoy

The stiff upper crust.

Patient babbles while

Psychiatrist just listens

But pays him no mind.

He knows electronics

And he often manages

To be her laptop.

Do I stand a chance?

No, you simply do not fit

Into my belle curve.

White House hesitates.

Is it procrastination?

Perhaps Tom's DeLay?

Creative Chinese

Chef prepares lo mein 6 ways,

Uses his noodle.

Unemployed actor

With a demolition firm

Now brings down the house.

Guitarist offers

True love with a smile. Is she

Stringing me along?

Committees of fat

Japanese legislators

Ignore their Diet.

Nurse fails to draw blood

Even with thinnest needle,

Pokes my arm in vain.

Paul Treatman

Old school principals,

They say, never die—merely

Lose their faculties.

Basic unit of

Laryngitis might only

Be one hoarsepower.

Paul Treatman

Teacher sends class to

School eye doc, class returns as

Dilated pupils.

Champion race horse

Gets extensive dental work,

Then wins triple crown.

Black widow spider

Invites her husband: Browse my

Attractive website.

Conga dancer and

Hula dancer, each truly

Asset to music.

Double hernia?

Operate, doctor, but take

Care of tenderloins.

Lawyer wins award

For client in the courtroom,

Wraps up suitcase.

Lady buys diet

Program, becomes very fat,

Laments: Go figure.

Precious rock store

Closed by the police. Owners

Took much for granite.

Paul Treatman

Beset by boredom,

Husband seeks other woman,

Breaks monogamy.

Accident victim

Insists on sewing own wound.

Doc says suture self.

Paul Treatman

Crazed cowboy enters

Mental hospital, singing

Home, home on derange.

Guests at reception

Hunger for the wedding cake

In all its Splenda.

New MD.'s consult

Via their P.C.'s, call it

Their own intern net.

Computer shop posts

Sign on front door advising

Out for a quick byte.

Nudist colony

Holds dance, folks enjoy waltzing

And a strip polka.

Reluctant chicken

Escapes from slaughterer, who

Then tries to pullet.

Sheep rancher would like

To expand his herd, but he

Suffers lack of ram.

Measurement system

Changing. As Europe does, we

Follow the liter.

Paul Treatman

Mommy pig would not

Let farmer near her, but

The baby piglet.

Want multiple birth?

Take some ripe eggs and mix with

Loads of poppy seed.

Actor at brothel

Pays madam for the chance to

Star in passion play.

In animal heaven,

Who is actually in charge?

Reigning cats and dogs.

Luxury auto

Sales decline, and that is how

The Mercedes Benz.

Dogs run wild aboard

Ship, creating havoc all

Over the poop deck.

Scientists study

Auto exhausts, have to squirt

One "Pour Homme" per fume.

Pregnant lady dives

Into heated pool to prove

She lacks cold fetus.

Farmer with poor sight

Digs into flower garden

Seeking a light bulb.

Male sex offenders

Sentenced by judge to a

Penile colony.

Allergic lady

Declines to enter woodshop

Because she saw dust.

Acupuncturist

Sticks me with nineteen needles—

These are jabs well done.

Ailing baseball star

Throws balls, strikes, catches flies and

Plays at fever pitch.

Ball park fan

With same mustard on hot dogs—

Case of Dijon vu?

Thief steals painting from

Museum, gets arrested,

Tells judge cops framed him.

Joey Adams said

An ascot was something a

Donkey must sleep on.

Paul Treatman

Seeking huge profits,

Real crazy for the money,

Partners were doughnuts.

Escaping from flood,

Pregnant woman considers

A Row vs. Wade.

Cops just arrested

Energizer Bunny, who was

Charged with battery.

Football player at

Barbecue anxious to

Handle the pigskin.

Writer accused of

Plagiarism finally

Is booked by police.

Cyclist gives up race—

Bicycle wears out

And remains two-tired.

Paul Treatman

Physicists who are

Catholic, do they attend

A Molecule Mass?

When tourists could not

Find Lenin's Tomb, they surmised

A communist plot.

Paul Treatman

⌒

Musician's girl friend

Never tells the truth, but he

Still loves his lyre.

Heard from fisherman's

Daily catch: Frankly, scallop,

I don't give clam.

Paul Treatman

⁓

Ornithologist

Loves his many birds, although

One is raven mad.

Ophthalmologists

Conferring at a meeting

Can see eye to eye.

Paul Treatman

Musician drives through

France, scaring pedestrians,

Honking his French horn.

Retired admiral

Launches new career as a

TV anchorman.

Jewish prisoners

Seek freedom, hungry,

Eat locks and escape.

Dog chases cat in

The forest, but finally

Barks up the wrong tree.

Wealthy investor

In trendy restaurant

Gives waiter good tips.

Gardener ruined

His patch of herbs because he

Ignored sage advice.

Young groom flusters at

The alter, realizes

He was miss-taken.

Matador boasting

His exploits to friends, who say

He is full of bull.

Paul Treatman

Missing my kinfolk,

I decide to take off,

Go to Antilles.

Sold-out throng welcomes

Renowned spiritual head,

Shouts Hello Dalai.

Paul Treatman

~

Scurrilous campaign

Talk targeted by irate

TV denouncer.

Math expert checks

Chinese food, claims two thousand

Pounds of soup won ton.

Transvestite, a guy

Who likes eating and drinking

And to be Mary.

Gynecologist

Posts sign over the front door:

Now at your cervix.

Child says: Shakespeare wrote

Comedies, tragedies and

Hysterectomies.

Proctologist sign:

Please pay bill promptly because

We are in arrears.

3 Stooges throw pies

At one another. All of

Them always get creamed.

Scientist teaches

Insects to use language. Ever

See a spelling bee?

Paul Treatman

Wild candy maker:

Marshmallows extremely hard,

The peanut brutal.

Goliath's mom warns

Son not to play with David

Or he'll come home stoned.

Counterfeit painter

Has copy sold at high price,

Has brush with the law.

At North Pole workshop,

Each of Santa's elves known as

Subordinate Clauses.

Paul Treatman

New legislation

Stipulates air pollution

A mist-demeanor.

Famed dancer wears out

Many pairs of shoes as he

Taps to sole music.

Deliberately,

Man deposited money

On the River Bank.

Cattle rustler sought

By sheriff, decides he must

Take it on the lamb.

Paul Treatman

Court closes weekends

When judge declares he cannot

Allow Sunday suits.

Slaughterhouse butcher

Exits from refrigerator

So he can chill out.

Paul Treatman

Papparazzi claim

Shooting pictures of the famous

Is often a snap.

New York ball team hires

Barber to service the men,

That Yankee Clipper.

Londoner breaks with

Girl friend after spat, decides

He must leave her flat.

Chef tells silly jokes

On TV show, shrink says

He's a real crockpot.

Paul Treatman

Horticulturist

Happily removes weeds, plants seed,

Good sense of humus.

Income tax, sales tax,

Liquor tax, real estate tax,

How about thumb tax?

Girl falls in love with

Handsome flounder fisherman

Hook, line and stinker.

Itchy congregant

Rubs coin on synogogue wall,

Scratching his temple.

Paul Treatman

~

Police raid massage

Parlor. Masseuse rubbed someone

Famous the wrong way.

Girl goat to boy goat:

Yes, I shall go out with you

But please don't kid me.

Paul Treatman

Internet wizards!

Computer's first sign of age:

Loss of memory.

Job at nursery

Can lead a young graduate

To budding career.

Convict, behind bars,

Demands right to call lawyer

Using a cell phone.

Psychology class:

Do you remember Pavlov?

His name rings a bell.

Paul Treatman

Contractor on roof

Makes repairs, falls ill and so

Breaks down with shingles.

The trenchermen gulp

Down the heavy dinner that

Might well go to waist.

Paul Treatman

⁓

Anxious ladies crowd

A Victoria's Secret,

Concerned with hold-ups.

Eccentric wills all

To his collies. His fortune

Thus goes to the dogs.

Hungry astronaut

Enters space shuttle with food,

Enjoys a good launch.

Lady deposits

Loads of cash, teller exclaims

You can bank on it.

Paul Treatman

Ex-prisoner tries

Gardening, decides to turn

Over a new leaf.

Drunk empties bottle,

Becomes ill, staggers, falls, knows

Now the wrath of grapes.

Author Baudelaire,

Writing of a sexy lady,

Madam Ovary.

Run off, marry me!

Sorry, man, I canteloupe.

Oh, please, honeydew.

Paul Treatman

Egyptian princess

Goes to the Bank of the Nile

To get some prophet.

Men who always sleep

Through political speeches

Are called bulldozers.

Safe sex drive holds that

Condoms be used every

Conceivable occasion.

Hillbilly complains

His shotgun wedding was a

Case of wife or death.

Paul Treatman

To get on other side,

Chicken crossing road is

Poultry in motion.

Two egotists meet,

Exchange heated words and threats,

An I for an I.

Paul Treatman

Nome, warm in summer,

Cold in winter; do you like

Some baked Alaska?

Rejected lover

Jumps off a bridge in Paris.

Was he just in Seine?

Turtle crosses road

Seeking armor repair at

A new Shell station.

Wife pours coffee for

Husband, who complains bitterly,

Screams grounds for divorce.

Biblical Boaz,

Before choosing to marry,

Was clearly Ruthless.

They did not play cards

On the Ark because Noah

Was standing on the deck.

Paul Treatman

Microbiology lab

Posts warning sign on lab door:

Be careful, staph only.

Dancing cheek to cheek,

A romantic position,

A form of floor play.

Paul Treatman

Arriving at door,

He starts to sing, unable

Alas, to find key.

Shell fisherman, his

Catch so poor, and still he deigns

To become crabby.

Paul Treatman

Tales of blaze-setting,

Wackos now recorded in

Arson Hall of Flame.

Rating his singing

On one-to-ten scale, I must

Rate him a tenor.

Paul Treatman

He married three times,

Considered his number two

As a good mid-wife.

Dog hits age thirteen,

Loving master decides to

Make him Bark-Mitzvah.

Paul Treatman

~

Trailer truck breaks down

Spilling silverware cargo,

Many forks in road.

Sign at synogogue

Reads: Don't give up, Moses was

Once a basket case.

Vegetarian

Café: All we are saying

Is give peas a chance.

He just uses salacious

Material, never clean.

Isn't Howard Stern?

Paul Treatman

~

A new employee

In orange juice factory

Could not concentrate.

Man who fell into

Upholstery machine now

Fully recovered.

Paul Treatman

Muffler factory

Employees find job

Very exhausting.

Cabinet maker

Arrested by police

As counterfitter.

Paul Treatman

Want good pain relief?

Try acupuncture and you

Shall soon get the point.

Anatomical

Expert: "Half large intestine

Is semicolon."

Paul Treatman

New Year's, time runs out,

Get new calendar, the old

One's days numbered.

Number of call girls

Recruited by CIA

Work undercover.

Paul Treatman

English hunter seeks

Fun and game all day and night,

Ends wild goose chase.

Slip on peel and smack

The pavement, takes only a

Bananosecond.

Paul Treatman

The condemned man swings

In a tight noose until he

Gets the hang of it.

Distraught gambler plays

Poorly, loses heavily,

Plays not with full deck.

Paul Treatman

This oriental gent

Seldom drinks, yet at times

Tries to Taiwan on.

Nuclear worker

Starts losing his hair, claims he

Suffers from fallout.

Paul Treatman

Rich man builds lavish

Home for his doting mother—

Edifice complex.

Peg board players

Face off in Canada, each

Goes to Winnipeg.

Paul Treatman

Birdwatcher peers all

Day, not spotting any birds,

Having no egrets.

Dracula sits down

At a stylish restaurant,

Does not order stake.

My orthography

Suffers when medication

Gives me crazy spells.

She accepted her

Poet suitor, married him

For better or verse.

Paul Treatman

Construction worker

Tries to avoid lung disease

Asbestos he can.

Dad admonishes

Mischievous 8-year old, says

Behave and benign.

Paul Treatman

I tried to reach you

Once by mail, once by phone, as

A matter of fax.

Governor pardons

Convicted killer, who sighs

No noose is good noose.

Paul Treatman

Barber tries combing

Balding man's hair, says parting

Is such sweet sorrow.

Santa does not have

A candidate to vote for

While at the north poll.

Sir Lancelot's lame mount

Would often stumble and fall.

It was his knight mare.

Braggart tells about

His exploits with many girls.

He is so cocksure.

Paul Treatman

Norm finally fixed

His old gas barbecue grill

To his grate relief.

Sweaty coal miner

Covered with dust and dirt, says

That grime does not pay.

Paul Treatman

~

Sick, recovers, but,

Unexpectedly, he takes

A turn for the hearse.

Tourist, Amsterdam,

Cruising in red light district,

Gets himself in Dutch.

Paul Treatman

A brilliant con man

Defrauds a government and

Leaves Canada dry.

Fishing contest seeks

Man who baits hooks the fastest—

A master baiter.

Paul Treatman

New podiatrist

Makes home visits to patients

In his big toe truck.

978-0-595-39271-1
0-595-39271-7